Adventures of a Pangopup

All proceeds from this book go directly to pangolin conservation.

For Neill, for always championing my dreams. - T.T.
For Lisa, my younger daughter. - I.S.

Author: Terri Tatchell is a Canadian writer known for her Oscar-nominated work on 'District 9'. Her love for animals and allegory have united in the creation of the Endangered and Misunderstood series, giving the underdogs of endangered animals a lyrical voice filled with laughter, adventure and relatable themes.

Illustrator: Ivan Sulima graduated from the book graphics department of the Hyiv Polytechnic Institute and has worked as a children's book illustrator since 2010. His father Kostyantyn Sulyma and grandfather Petro Kozin are known Ukrainian artists.

FIRST EDITION
Canadian English
ISBN 978-1-9991022-4-1 (softcover)
ISBN 978-1-9991022-5-8 (hardcover)
ISBN 978-1-9991022-6-5 (PDF)
ISBN 978-1-9991022-7-2 (hardcover with jacket)

Published 2020 by
Fielding House Press
www.fieldinghousepress.com

FIELDING HOUSE PRESS

Adventures of a Pangopup

There was a little pangolin
whose name was Pangopup.
He rode upon his mother's tail
and dreamt of growing up.

He practiced all the pango ways
to keep so safe and sound,
yet Mother wouldn't let him leave
their burrow in the ground.

She said, "There's danger everywhere."
She said, "You are too small."
This made him rather angry so
he WHACKED their burrow wall.

She sighed, "This shows me that I'm right,
to keep you safe inside.
Now please be calm and let me teach
you how to duck and hide."

He thought that he was old enough
and planned to sneak away.
He'd learned his lessons extra well
and now deserved to play.

He waited for her SNORING sounds,
to know she was asleep.
Then slipped away - that naughty pup -
and didn't make a peep.

He crept outside and was SURPRISED!
The sun, it shone so bright!
See pangolins, they sleep all day
and venture out at night.

Because it took him by surprise,
he curled up in a ball.
Until he felt a little tap
and someone softly call,

"Oh Pangopup don't be afraid,
you're safe and sound with me!
Uncurl yourself, we'll have some FUN,
there's much for you to see!"

There was a pause and then a PUFF.
His best defence slipped out.
A noxious smell from his behind,
that made the creature shout:

"Why would you do that Pangopup?!
Don't waste your stink on me.
It's good to scare your enemies,
but I'm your friend, you see?"

When Pango peered out from his curl,
he spied a tiny deer,
who smiled at him with so much warmth,
that Pango lost his fear.

"My friends all call me Dik Dik deer,"
he heard the creature say.
"I have not seen you here before,
let's have some FUN today!"

So Pango rolled onto his feet
and beamed at his new friend.
"I'd LOVE to play with you outside!
This day can never end!"

They walked and talked,

and had some snacks.

They even had a swim.

And Pango met so many friends, who smiled and welcomed him.

Well, Dik Dik smiled and cocked his head.
"That's not exactly right.
I've kept us safe and sound, but now...
should we go find a FRIGHT?"

Poor Pangopup, he wasn't sure,
but wanted to be brave.
He hemmed and hawed for just a bit,
and then began to cave.

"Okay, why not? I'm up for that.
If there's a fright to find.
I'll just keep back and follow you
at first, if you don't mind?"

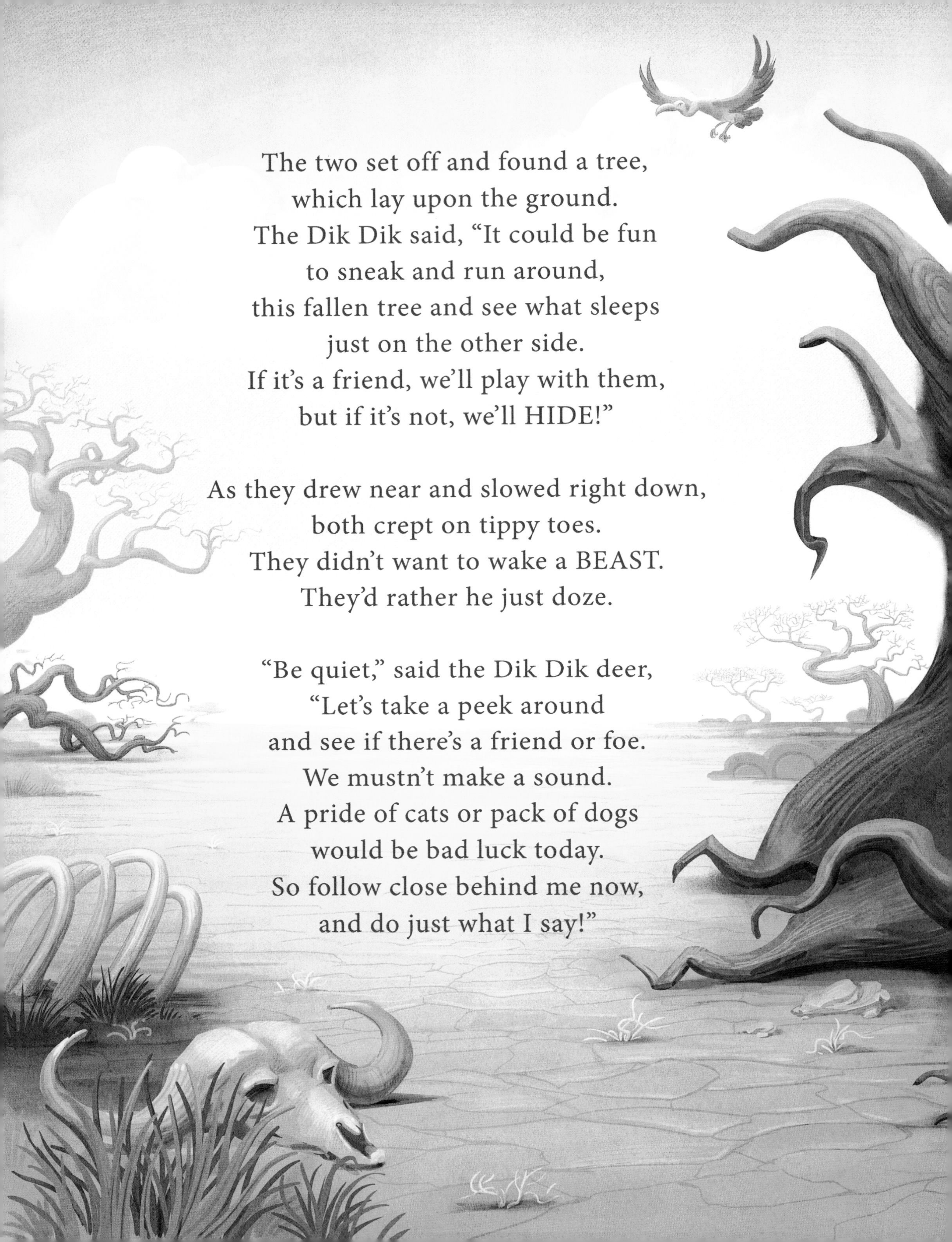

The two set off and found a tree,
which lay upon the ground.
The Dik Dik said, "It could be fun
to sneak and run around,
this fallen tree and see what sleeps
just on the other side.
If it's a friend, we'll play with them,
but if it's not, we'll HIDE!"

As they drew near and slowed right down,
both crept on tippy toes.
They didn't want to wake a BEAST.
They'd rather he just doze.

"Be quiet," said the Dik Dik deer,
"Let's take a peek around
and see if there's a friend or foe.
We mustn't make a sound.
A pride of cats or pack of dogs
would be bad luck today.
So follow close behind me now,
and do just what I say!"

Around that log, there was a FRIGHT,
far worse than any cat.
A GREAT BIG CREATURE wearing clothes!
It even had a HAT!

The Dik Dik deer just backed away,
but Pango was too SCARED.
He rolled up tight and held his breath
(In case his rear end flared).

Some moments passed and not a sound
from Dik Dik or that THING.
So Pango peeked outside his curl,
and it began to sing!

"Oh little tiny pangolin,
you rolled so close to me.
I think that I should scoop you up,
and take you home for tea."

That giant creature laughed out loud,
then STUFFED him in a SACK!
And started off towards its house
and didn't once look back.

If it had looked, it would have seen,
the Dik Dik running near.
He RAMMED his horns into its legs.
It SCREAMED in shock and fear.

And then it dropped the burlap sack
(Which was the Dik Dik's plan).
And Pangopup came rolling out,
then he and Dik Dik RAN!

They both were oh-so-terrified,
but Pango's legs were slow.
He saw a hole and ducked inside
and yelled: "DIK DIK, JUST GO!"

Well, Dik Dik really had no choice,
he knew he couldn't stay.
That angry thing had found a jeep.
He had to get AWAY!

So off he ran at LIGHTNING SPEED.
The jeep was not so quick.
And even though both got away,
the fright made Pango sick.

He waited till the sun went down,
to creep back to his house.
But on the way, he happened by
a tiny little mouse.

"Hello," the tiny mouse did squeak,
"I'm out alone tonight.
My family thinks that I'm too small.
But I don't think they're right."

Well, all that Pango wanted was
to get back home to mom.
But this small mouse was way too young.
She even sucked her THUMB!

He'd learned a thing or two that day,
felt wise beyond his years.
He sat with Mouse and shared his scare
and even shed some tears.

When he was done, he walked young Mouse,
back to her family's nest.

Then found his burrow in the ground,
and told his mom the rest.

He told her why he ran away,
and that he'd had some fun.
But that he still had much to learn
and how he couldn't RUN!

His mom, she sat and listened well,
and held him OH-SO-TIGHT.

Then placed him back upon her tail,
and there he slept all night.

ENDANGERED AND MISUNDERSTOOD?

An endangered animal is in danger of not existing and needs our protection. There are eight species of pangolins that range from vulnerable to critically endangered, and the main predator of the pangolin is humans. Pangolins are the most trafficked animal in the world, which means they are sold illegally more than any other animal on Earth. Who would want to buy an illegal pangolin? Well, here is where the misunderstood part comes in! There is an incorrect belief that pangolin scales can be used as medicine. But did you know pangolin scales are keratin, which is the same material as your fingernails? Fingernails would make terrible medicine, wouldn't they?! The more people learn about the pangolin, the safer the pangolin will be!

1. Baby pangolins are called pangopups.
2. Pangolins walk on their hind legs using their tail and arms for balance!
3. Pangolins are great at smelling but not so great at seeing or hearing.
4. Pangolins have more vertebrae than any other animal.
5. Pangolins don't have any teeth!
6. Pangolins swallow stones to grind up their food.
7. Pangolin tongues are sticky and often longer than their bodies.
8. Pangolins can constrict their ears and nostrils to keep ants out while they eat.
9. Pangolins are covered in keratin scales, which are the same material as your fingernails.
10. There are eight different species of pangolins; four Asian and four African.

1.
The tiny dik-diks mate for life.

2.
Dik-diks mark their territory with tears, urine and feces.

3.
A dik-dik nose is prehensile, which means it can be used to grab things.

4.
Dik-diks don't need to drink water. They get enough from their food.

5.
None of the four species of dik-diks are endangered. Yay!

Endangered Misunderstood

FIVE WAYS TO HELP THE PANGOLIN

1. Teach someone an interesting pangolin fact!
2. Learn how to draw a pangolin. Paint each scale however you want!
3. Have an endangered animal birthday party. Give pangolin books as presents!
4. Ask if you can do a school project on the pangolin.
5. Don't ever ever EVER eat a pangolin!

For complimentary songs, story time videos, activities and more visit:
endangeredandmisunderstood.com

Printed in Great Britain
by Amazon

74573502R00020